THIS PAW PATROL STORYBOOK BELONGS TO

....

First published in the United States 2023 by Penguin Random House
This edition published in Great Britain 2023 by Farshore
An imprint of HarperCollins*Publishers*
1 London Bridge Street, London SE1 9GF
www.farshore.co.uk

HarperCollins*Publishers*
Macken House, 39/40 Mayor Street Upper,
Dublin 1, D01 C9W8, Ireland

Written by Frank Berrios
Illustrated by MJ Illustrations

ISBN 978 0 00 853721 0
Printed in UK
001

A CIP catalogue record for this title is available from the British Library.

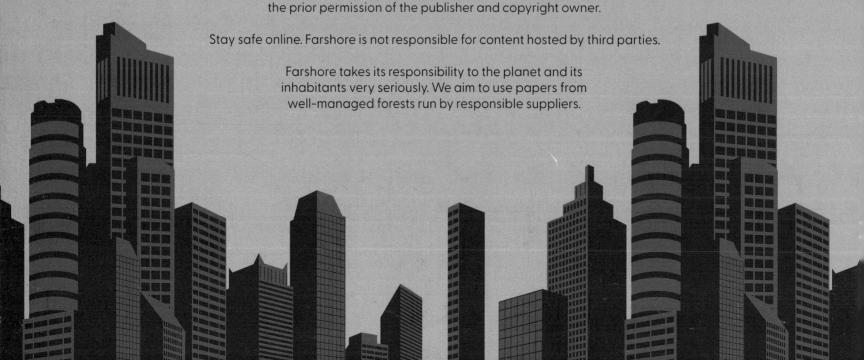

MIGHTY MOVIE STORYBOOK

It was another busy day in Adventure City for the PAW Patrol – they had just finished fighting a fire at a scrapyard.

"We're just glad there's not too much damage," said Ryder, after the owners thanked the team.

While the pups cleaned up, Chase learned that someone had stolen a giant electromagnet from the scrapyard.

Later, everyone in Adventure City prepared to watch a meteor shower. Everyone except the scientist Victoria Vance, also known as Vee. She had stolen the giant electromagnet for her plan to pluck a magical meteor out of the sky.

"My latest invention, the Meteor Magnet, will grab one of those meteors and gently deliver it to my doorstep," said Vee, recording a video.

Back at the Pup Tower, Ryder introduced the team to the Junior Patrollers: Nano, Mini and Tot. "They're working on their astronomy merit badges, so I invited them to watch the meteor shower with us," he said.

"I don't know about this Junior Patroller thing," mumbled Liberty.

"Don't write them off just because they're small!" replied Skye.

Little did the pups know, they were in danger. Vee had lost control of the meteor and it was heading straight for Adventure City!

"Everybody out of the street!" yelled Chase. "You need to take cover!"

The meteor smashed into the tower, ripped through the street and landed on the ground as a meteorite.

"It's giving off a strange energy pulse," said Ryder. "Let's find out what's going on."

Everyone knew that Vee had caused the crash thanks to her video. She was quickly arrested and put in the Adventure City Jail, where she soon made a new friend.

"Hello, roomie," said the archrival of the PAW Patrol – Mayor Humdinger!

Ryder and the pups moved to a new aircraft carrier, where they ran tests on the mysterious meteorite.

"We'll leave it to scan overnight and see what we can learn tomorrow," said Ryder.

Later that night, while the pups were sleeping, Skye was woken up by a strange noise. She went to the lab and lightly touched the meteorite. It fell apart! Then the crystal core split into seven shards.

When Skye took hold of one of the glowing shards, she began to float!
The crystal attached itself to her collar and, suddenly, she could fly!
She accidentally punched through a metal wall and woke the other pups up.
"What's going on?" asked Ryder.
"I think I've got … superpowers!" replied Skye.

One by one, the pups approached the crystals, which attached themselves to their collars. They instantly had superpowers! Marshall could create fireballs, Chase learned he had super speed, while Zuma transformed into water. Rocky was a walking magnet and Rubble could become a wrecking ball. But Liberty wasn't sure what her superpower was yet. "It's like these crystals amplify something about you," she said.

"Now that we're super, we're going to need a new name," said Rubble.
"How about the Mighty Pups?" suggested Ryder. The pups loved it!

The Mighty Pups even made the news!

"Now we know that superheroes are real," said Sam Stringer. "They've arrived in Adventure City and they call themselves the Mighty Pups! Thanks to the superpowers contained in that mysterious meteorite, the Mighty Pups are truly unstoppable."

Vee watched the newscast from jail. "That was my meteorite! They should be my superpowers," she cried.

"We'll help you get out of here if you promise to share some of those superpowers with me," said Humdinger.

"It's a deal," said Vee.

They escaped through a secret tunnel which ran down through a toilet. Yuck!

Back on the aircraft carrier, Liberty decided to train the new recruits. "Are you three puffballs serious about joining the PAW Patrol?" she asked. They all cheered yes. "Then I'm going to turn you into lean, mean, fluffy little rescue machines!"

Meanwhile, Vee planned to use Humdinger's jet to lure the pups to her. She threw some snacks into one of the jet's engines and called Ryder's PupPad for help.

"Mayday, mayday!" yelled Vee. "We need immediate assistance!"

Ryder answered the call. "Skye, I need you to fly up there and carry that plane down safely," he said. "Are you up for it?"

"I'm a Mighty Pup. I was made for this!" said Skye.

Skye quickly caught up to the damaged jet. But when Vee stole her collar, she realised it was a trick! Vee, Humdinger and the kittens jumped out of the plane.

"Ryder, come in – this is Skye," she said. "It was a trap! They stole my crystal! I've got no powers and the plane is going down."
"Skye, we're clearing a runway. Set a course for Main Street," Ryder replied.
Marshall handled crowd control while Rubble patched up a hole in the street. Then Chase marked the runway with flares.

Skye was able to land safely, but she was disappointed not to have her powers anymore – it was fun to fly without her helicopter.
"I'd do anything to get that crystal back," she told Chase.

Back at her observatory, Vee attached Skye's crystal to her necklace.
"I've finally got enough power to catch all the meteors I want.
I'll be the greatest scientist in history!"

Back on the aircraft carrier, Skye made up her mind. "If I'm going to get my crystal back, I'm going to need all the power I can get," she said, attaching the other pups' crystals to her collar. "I'll have them back before anyone knows they are gone!"

Skye found Vee at the observatory. But Vee trapped her in a force field and stole the rest of her crystals! She used her new superpowers to pull dozens of meteors towards Earth.

"Stop! People could get hurt!" said Skye.

"I tried to do things the right way, but I was swept aside and laughed at," replied Vee. "I promised myself I'd never let anyone make me feel small ever again!"

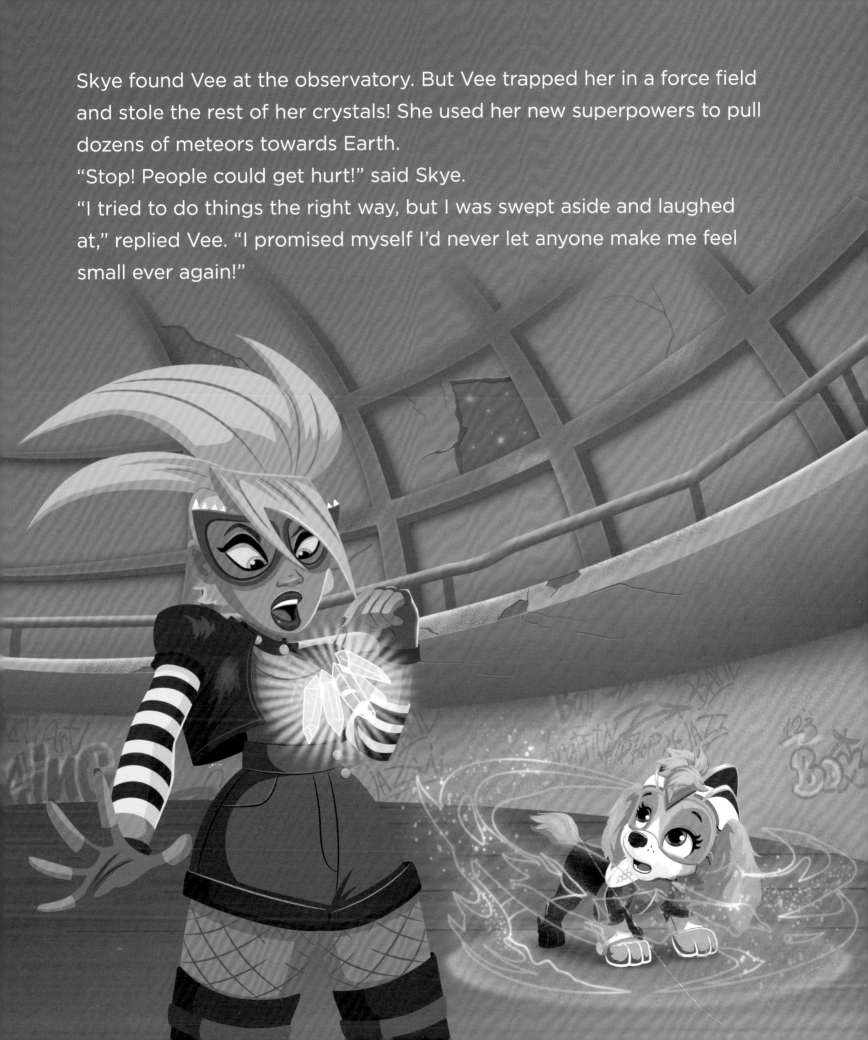

"I know what it's like to feel small. You have to work twice as hard as everyone else just to prove you belong," said Skye. "That's why I risked everything to get my crystal back. But all I did was make things worse for my friends."

Just then, Humdinger arrived. "One of those crystals is mine," he said.
"Ugh. Fine. A deal's a deal," said Vee.
Humdinger snatched the crystal and began to grow and grow!
"Now if you'll excuse me, I have to pay a visit to
the PAW Patrol," he said.

Without their superpowers, the PAW Patrol had to go back to basics.

The team raced out to face Humdinger.

"Spread out and don't get stepped on," said Ryder.

Before long, Humdinger had them cornered!

"Looks like it's the end of the road, PAW Patrol!" he said.

Thankfully, Nano, Mini and Tot weren't far away.

"The Junior Patrollers are on a roll!" yelled Mini as he and Tot used a crane to grab onto Humdinger's moustache. They raced up Humdinger's nose, which gave Marshall enough time to take the crystal out of his jacket pocket. The pups were mighty once more!

The Junior Patrollers had saved the day! Humdinger shrank back down to normal size and was taken to jail. After that, the Junior Patrollers helped Zuma free Skye and get the rest of the crystals back from Vee. Then Liberty discovered her superpower!

"I'm stretchy! I mean, how did I not think of that?" she said. "I'm a sausage dog. I'm already stretched out in real life!"

When Ryder learned that the meteors were still on their way to Earth, he quickly came up with a plan.

"Skye, I need you to fly up there and destroy as many of those meteors as you can," said Ryder.

"I'll give it everything I've got!" replied Skye.

"You'd better take all the power you can get," said Chase. He and the rest of the PAW Patrol gave Skye their crystals.

"No pup is too small!" shouted Skye as she punched the meteors away.
Adventure City was saved!
"Let's hear it for Skye and the Mighty Pups!" cheered the crowd.